OLD MAN MARLEY

The Greatest Un-Sagely
Sage from Everywhere and Nowhere

WRITTEN BY: AMEL ZAHID
ILLUSTRATIONS BY: ANUM ZAHID

www.writeandreleasepublishing.com

A NOTE FROM THE AUTHOR

Old Man Marley knocked on my heart's door a few years ago, bringing with him his stories. Writing them out brought me deep healing and joy. Seeing how much it helped me and those around me, I am now ready to share these stories with the world. My hope is to inspire a search for real healing and real freedom from our false sense of who we are and from the pain that this causes us. The effort here is to draw attention to meaning and bring the echoes of the questions to the foreground of our conscious thought process: Who are we, what are we doing and where are we going, really?

The stories are written very simply for anyone to enjoy at their level - children of any age or size. Each story stands on its own with no chronological order and can be read independently or in sequence.

A positive word or prayer to restore hope is all one can give to anyone faced with challenges. This is a book of positive words - a prayer almost. Leaving with a hope that the reader will be restored in finding their true essence, peace and what's essential in these very difficult times that humanity faces collectively.

For my parents, Zahid and Ruby,
and my son, Mekaal - my world in sum.

May the Marley in you thrive …

TABLE OF CONTENTS

INTRODUCING OLD MAN MARLEY

Old Man Marley is not anyone you know but perhaps everyone you know. I guarantee it. He was born old. He is not a white man nor a black man. He is neither Gandalf nor Dumbledore. He is eccentric and extremely moody. He belongs everywhere. He has zero respect for the rules of the English language, or any language or any rules for that matter! All he cares about is, communicating his unfettered thoughts.

Marley turns the world upside down, takes it apart at times, and rearranges it to fit his story, to help provide perspective and shed some light onto things he finds contradictory, as would you. Above all, he communicates wisdom in a way that would hope to warm the hearts of those who read it, perhaps sow some seeds of deeper thinking, and spread some smiles and laughter along the way.

I am sharing the stories now because I have enough "dirt" on him. For the skeptic, the eye-rollers, the horse-before-the-cart putters—these stories are not for you or maybe you need them the most. The rest, enjoy the pun, matter-of-fact play on words, and the twisting of the arms of science and logic while conveying wisdom all for spreading some light-hearted humor and perspective.

THE YOUNG OLD MAN

Old Man Marley was an only child insofar as one could consider themselves a child of time, but as you and I commonly understand, he had two brothers. A younger-older brother and an older-younger brother. One could never tell who was younger or older than Marley — sometimes Marley couldn't tell either. But that didn't bother him. He thought that was an irrelevant matter, as long as he had his next of kin next to him.

You see, age for Marley, was a matter of how "lived" you were. The real age then was counted by the number of big or small decisions each person made over their lives. And so it was for Marley, that the bigger the decisions a person made, the older they were, and the fewer and smaller decisions a person made, the younger they were. Then you could be a perfectly young-old person or a perfectly old-young person or any permutation thereof — young-young or old-old.

It was only natural that Everyone often wondered how old Marley really was. He certainly looked all his years and seemed to be making a lot of big decisions of-late. They knew all too well by now that asking Marley wouldn't get them a straightforward response so they had to find some other way.

Incidentally, it was his birthday and Everyone thought that would be the perfect occasion to find out. Why, one could simply count the number of candles Marley would have on his cake! So they all got dressed in their best clothes and went to wish Marley a very Happy Birthday indeed.

Once there, they were all surprised to see, Marley had only one candle on his cake. Just one. Everyone tallied that number with each other to affirm if they had indeed got the count right. One. They counted again to double-check.

They circumambulated the cake to see if they had missed any others that were perhaps hidden from view, on the other side. For how could Marley be only a year old! That made no sense to them at all. So they did what they had to do and ultimately asked Marley: "Marley Old Man, why do you only have one candle on your cake? Won't you tell us finally how old you are?"

To this Marley responded with his characteristic age-defying dazzling smile and a sheen to his eyes so bright, only a kid with a candy bar could beat.

"You see, Sillies, I am one year older and younger today and therefore, I celebrate only with one candle!"

"How can you be older and younger at the same time?!" responded Everyone, "And what about all the other years that came before? Who will count them?"

Marley shook his head dismissively.

"At this moment, I am one year older than last year, and I am one year younger than next year, as I am every year today. As for the years gone by, they have gone by...if they wanted to count they would have stayed with me, like this present moment — that never leaves me or you for that matter."

With this, Marley blew his one and only candle and embraced Everyone in one giant hug, so grateful for the present moment and Everyone's presence in it - young, old, or any permutation thereof. What mattered most was that they were all here and now.

DUSTY — THE WIFE

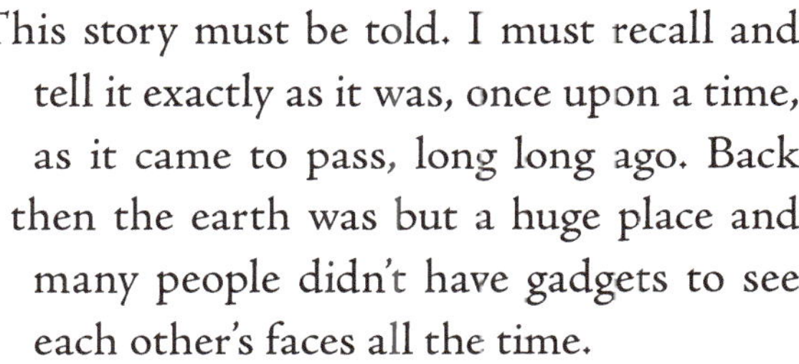

This story must be told. I must recall and tell it exactly as it was, once upon a time, as it came to pass, long long ago. Back then the earth was but a huge place and many people didn't have gadgets to see each other's faces all the time.

Please keep a tissue at hand and have a seat, for this is a very sad story:

In the days when Old Man Marley wasn't as old, nor as wise, but a fool and a younger older man, he sought a partner in life.

Now he did not ask for much. He wanted someone who would fit the job description loosely: make tea and cookies, care for him, file for tax returns, know how to play chess, be a polyglot, a polymath, supremely beautiful and the list of course went on. But more or less, someone he could come home to, and would help make his home a home.

With what he had in mind, he knew only he could create such a person, for where could he find one exactly as the mind perceived her to be?

So he went about fashioning a woman out of dust!

She was beautiful. And very down to earth of course. Grounded in values and not valuables. And so he loved her very much.

Sometimes they would argue here and there. She of course was a creationist and believed she was created with a specific purpose, by loving hands, out of dust, and to dust she would return, as would all of mankind. Old Man would tell her, pedantically, how that was only true for her and not him or mankind: That he is in fact a better-looking child of monkeys and that there was such a thing as evolution and revolution that caused the society to be as it is. But they were able to lovingly resolve their conflict when she called him "Monkey Buns" and he "Dusty".

Beyond their discourses, she would tell him jokes, and he would laugh much in the evenings.

She kept herself beautiful by sprinkling all the dust she'd gathered in the house onto her, in her hair, and all around. And the house stayed clean. She would even do the taxes for him. By Golly, Marley was the happiest man monkeying around on earth as it was. But as it goes, much wants more and so did Old Man Marley.

As the months went by, and there weren't many, Old Man noticed how she'd grown on him. She was now twice the size she was when he made her. She had gathered too much dust when he wasn't paying attention. So it happened, as it does over time.

But he kept his expectations of her in a jar and saved each thought as a droplet. Many droplets began to form a pool. And as she grew so did the pool of his expectations. One fine day, Marley, raised with a great sense of entitlement and self-importance, decided to let Dusty know about all his unmet expectations. So, he found her upstairs humming to herself serenely, rubbing dust in her face.

Marley opened the jar — now carrying a huge pool. The pool spread around Dusty quickly, as we all know how unmanageable unmet expectations can be. Seeing what surrounded her now, she

couldn't help but dissolve in it. And disappear just like that she did — without much justification or protest.

Old Man thought she'd come back but she had already drowned in the pool of expectations, being made of dust. Poor Marley only later realized his mistake, and sobbed for life holding his hat, wheezing and coughing as he wailed: "Dusty!.... DUSTY!........DUSTYEeeee!"

Sigh!

What a mess lay before him. There would never be another like her for she was the only one he had made. He would never make another.

Moral of the story:
If your partner is made of dust,
do not place them in a pool — you fool!

The Two-Storied House

Once again and once upon a time, Old Man Marley bought a house. It was as nice a house as they come. It had two floors, a nice yard, and a quaint pool.

Everyone was curious about the beautiful things Old Man Marley would get to furnish the house. So he did and invited Everyone over.

Driven by sheer curiosity of the unknown, of course, Everyone came. To their surprise, the house was done beautifully, with tapestries from exotic places, lamps from brilliant places, paintings from vibrant places, and porcelain from far-off places. They all approved of it in unison. They thought that perhaps they could all relate to the very expensive items and that now they could finally be friends. They said:

"Great going, Marley!"

"Yes, what a great job you've done, Old Man! What unique stuff do you have here, we have similar things also. Come shall we talk about them?"

Marley, very pleased with himself, then gestured to show the upstairs —Everyone followed him up.

There it was: the very same tapestries, the very same lamps, and the very same everything, exactly as what was downstairs and placed exactly in the same manner!

But why?

Everyone was so confused. Perplexed. Confounded. Bamboozled even!

Their experience of normalcy stood torn apart yet again at the hands of this Old Man, who played two, three, four— all at once! Again. Or so they felt. Played on.

Everyone looked at Marley for an explanation. Marley of course, not seeing this as a prompt continued to smile, blinking occasionally as was the function of the eyelid. Finally, Everyone broke the silence with:

"What is this? Why is everything the same?"

To this Marley stood with a great calm, attributable heretofore only to the lotus plant upon the surface of a still lake. Swinging his hand forward and back in a sage-like fashion, he responded:

"As above, so below."

Everyone was so puzzled, and tried to be polite and said: "Excuse us. Yes, that is what we are saying. It is below as it is above!"

To which Marley clapped with excitement as if something just got resolved,

"Great! So you see it too now! We can finally have dinner!"

And then gesturing to both floors he asked:

"Where would you like to eat?"

Everyone sighed in great exasperation. They could choose where to eat, but what they ate would be the same, down to the tellicherry peppercorn seasoning. Did their choice matter?

Of course, it did!

Upstairs was the better view!

Old Man Marley's House

Marley Dusts

What is simple for some may be complicated for others. And those who don't know another's story can never know another's day-to-day moments of glory. Glory, because the minutest of tasks for one person can pose an insurmountable challenge for another.

For Old Man Marley, the hardest thing to do was dusting! For he wept so much that his voice would turn hoarse and his eyes would well up with the tears, held in limbo, waiting to be shed but not quite ready yet. Everyone would find it hard to recognize Old Man Marley. Old Man Marley this way would only make an appearance once or twice a year, and Everyone would know that he had been severely dusting.

Oh Boy. He'd weep so much that he'd sneeze and gurgle and bend over wheezing and hissing. Then he'd sit in the corner pressing his thumbs into his eyes to stop the tears from flowing. Then he'd lie down straight holding his hand unto his heart, wheezing for his one true love, Dusty, his wife. For all the dust reminded him of her when now she was no longer.

But this story is not about Dusty. That one has already been told. Many times over and over. This story is about how Marley overcame and accomplished the act of dusting when each particle rose into swirling whirls bombarded by the random action of the gaseous particles that make up what we call air. They took the form of a beautiful woman, almost telling Marley to suck in his tummy and sit up straight, the way she always told him to do.

And so each particle beat him down with beautiful memories of yore, but he would persist despite the tears with his fuzzy duster and his hair neatly covered, gagging, weeping, coughing.

Everyone knew never to mention the word dust in front of Marley, for that was enough for the grieving man to relive it all over again. Even at burials, people would avoid using the phrase: "Ashes to ashes, dust to dust." Instead, they'd just say: "Ashes to ashes," and disperse quickly, avoiding eye contact with Marley at all costs.

So it happened that Everyone saw Old Man Marley headed up the aisle to buy a new duster. He wept so much at the checkout line that Everyone offered to dust for him for free. But obviously, he felt very possessive about the act and let Everyone know that all the dust lying around was only his to clean and not for anyone else. When people insisted, he took out his Tommy gun and told them to back off! (You see, where he lived, there were no gun control laws, yet.)

So then Marley would finish dusting and it took him a good few days to get the job done, but he knew facing it all and going through the process was the only way to his freedom. His heart bubbled with joy remembering how she would call him a lazy oaf for not screwing in the lightbulb properly and in time for the guests to arrive, or how she'd sing for him a dusty song about a dusty road.

Once Marley was done, he ran about town hugging Everyone for the love that was left in him after all the dust was cleared. Only then did Everyone know that their very own old man was back to bringing magic back to their ordinary days.

ON MATTERS PERTAINING TO THE SOLE

Once upon a time, Old Man Marley woke up with that feeling you get where everything seems fine on the surface but deep down you know something is wrong but you can't exactly put your finger on it. Except in Marley's case, it was his toe. He could not put his toe on it.

Marley was soon to find his favorite and *only* pair of shoes had gone missing!

Now you can only imagine the distress of a man so accustomed to finding his usual pair right where he left it before going to bed — for the past seventeen years! His feet had known no other shoes.

But today, the shoes had walked off on their own to find new adventures maybe? The sense of betrayal was great and so was the sense of self-doubt. Did his shoes leave him because his feet had become too smelly? As that thought struck, Marley quickly proceeded to smell his feet. They were ok. So he stood there wiggling his toes wondering what to do next.

Everyone soon found lost-and-found fliers featuring a pair of really old worn shoes. They were stuck everywhere — against lampposts, on buses, trains, cats, dogs, babies even. Everyone very soon knew they had a situation — a Marley situation — and were forced to offer their opinions on the matter.

"Old man, why don't you consider buying new shoes? There are so many different kinds out there and so many colors to choose from!"

"Hey, Marley, if you want you can dip your foot in shoe-making stuff, and a shoe can simply be wrapped around your foot the way you want — like one of those DIY shoes! Why don't you save yourself from the trouble of looking?"

For Marley though, one did not simply buy a new pair like some random consumer good. Some goods are just greater than that. What was far truer than true was that no shoes could buy more Marleys — even if they were willing to pay a million dollars a piece — a billion even. The father of economics couldn't tell us everything. In fact, there is very little about the true nature of things that he has ever conveyed, especially where it concerned soles. No, that was an entirely different matter.

Naturally, then, the thought of new shoes frightened Marley, just as the thought of new Marleys would frighten old shoes! The break-in and the discomfort one had to go through were inevitable before they could be trusted to carry him on every walk and every trail of life without so much as a squeak.

It was true: shoes that walk away seldom find their way back.

Soon Marley understood that walking around barefoot made him look very unprofessional. And of course, his feet hurt. He understood that no matter how much he looked for his old pair, he would not find them, or they him. This he was able to ascertain through an insta-harm post made by his old shoes. They were up in Bermuda, way out of their box, digging their heels into the sand and basking in the sun as if they were a bunch of flippant flip-flops — instead of the loafers they really were!

Moral of the story:
Never take a sole for granted.

Old Man Meets New Year

Old Man Marley woke up on the first day of the first month of the new year and pulled apart the curtains. He took his first deep breaths into the new year, put on his overalls, picked up his paint bucket, and went about repainting the world without further ado. For if the world needed to be changed, he was going to do it.

At this point, Everyone was fast asleep next to their New Year's resolutions that they had been working on the night before — same as you and me.

But, Marley was painting the tree leaves blue and the trunk a bright red by now. He went around and spray-painted the sky a hue of lavender and orange and then dipped the oceans in a beautiful tone of pink. He polka-dotted the clouds with chocolate chip brown and bright blue! The grass was zebra striped and zebra's stripes were now violet hearts! Just like that. What a way to do things. And what a lot Marley had done!

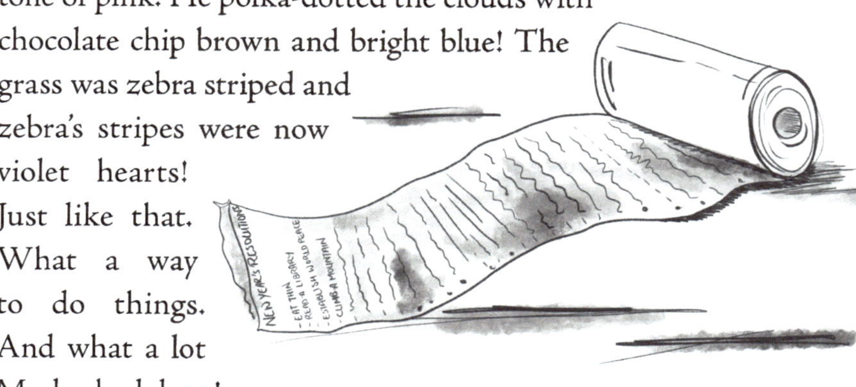

Each building and car that Marley came across, he colored them all a neutral blue to balance out the brightness of newly colored nature. This was important because Old Marley was above all a man of excellent taste.

Very satisfied with a job thoroughly done, Marley lay in the, now, purple snow and made snow angels before retreating. He was overjoyed with the splish splash of color everywhere. Finally, he took out his list of New Year's resolutions and crossed off the first item on his list:

1) Re-paint the world without further ado.

Everyone that now woke up had to rub their eyes a few times to address what met their eyes for all that was taken for granted was there no more or not as their mind was accustomed to seeing, or ready for. You can only imagine the choice they faced of having to live in a world, not knowing what color ought what be. Especially the traffic lights.

They knew by now of course, (and the snow angels provided evidence) that it had to be the Old Man's doing for only he could whip up such magic overnight. They found Marley dipping his hands in red paint and so he was caught — red-handed.

"Marley, Old Man, why are you doing this to us?" said Everyone as they approached Marley for a solution.

Feeling quite guilty Marley started off with:

"The simple explanation is this: I had run out of paint…"

Marley paused before adding,

"…but maybe I can still put a mustache on all of your faces? … If you can line up here…"

With this, he reached into a black paint bucket, and dipped his brush in, ready to draw.

With a great sigh of exasperation, Everyone exclaimed:

"No! We don't want mustaches! or bunny ears! We want everything as before. Why do you mess with everything?"

…They wanted the sky a blue, the grass a green, and zebras with their stripes of black and white.

Marley's wrinkly face full of kind consideration turned suddenly mirthful. He stood up and took a giant hose, and laughed so hard it shook the earth. Delightfully he exclaimed:

"Now that is an easy fix!"

And as Marley let the water gush out of the hose he yelled:

"Happy Old New Year Every Bodies!"

You see, he had used washable paints — not the permanent kind. So he washed everything down to reveal the original color of everything.

Marley smiled. He was happy to have solved one of the biggest problems facing mankind even if he was the one who created it in the first place, like most of us do.

Everyone thanked Marley for returning their world to the way they always knew it was. They all started their new year with a profound sense of gratitude —appreciating what they had a lot more now than when it was just there — down to the zebra's stripes. They found joy in the ordinary.

But there was nothing ordinary about the next item on Marley's agenda. For item number two on his list of New Year's resolutions read:

2) Yodel all the way to the moon

And so Old Man Marley entered the address for the Moon on his GPS, tightened his aviator-goggles, and off he went. Yodeling. And there he remains to this day, which is the second day of the first month of the new year. If you found a time and place to step outside the worldly din you might even hear him yodel.

Can you hear him?

How about now?

Now?

Right Side Up

Once upon a time, Everyone woke up and found Old Man Marley hanging upside down from a nearby tree. He seemed to be very comfortable there, and in fact, he was enjoying a cup of tea by himself, while reading the newspaper — wrong side up, too. Everyone tried to find a reasonable explanation for Marley's actions. It was marvelous to see how their good intentions played out.

One said:

"He is probably just hanging out to dry after swimming in the lake."

Another said:

"He's trying out a new fitness regime... I know there is a guru in town from the distant land of India who teaches doing things this way. It activates the upside-down-hanging chakra..."

Everyone nodded in approval. Everyone liked this neatly rounded-off explanation best because they did not understand it and it was nicely complicated. Yet another said:

"Oh no! Surely this time, he has lost it. We all knew he was heading there anyway."

Another said:

"Why don't we just ask him so he can explain it himself?"

A very long silence followed. Everyone appreciated the idea as logically sound and reasonable, but no one had the courage to walk up to an upside-down-hanging-tea-drinking-newspaper-reading man and interrupt him. They thought it wasn't the politest thing to do — interrupt someone so engrossed in something. It was definitely simpler to find conclusions on assumptions.

Finally, someone approached Marley and asked him:

"Marley, old man, what is the matter with you? Why are you hanging upside-down like so, when you could be easily doing the very same things sitting in a good old armchair, right-side-up?"

To this Marley responded, while still hanging upside down from the tree:

"I am the right side up now as well. Who told you I was the wrong side up? Who knows what's what these days anyway? Do you? From my perspective, all of you are on the wrong side!"

Now Everyone was just left dumbfounded. No one had ever questioned their right-side-up-ness before. They had no idea what to say next. One of them raised a finger and tried to utter some words but none came out. And so they all left.

THE T.F.B

So it happened once that Old Man Marley felt the need for a true friend. Sure there was Everyone. But a true friend, the Old Man thought, would be one that would always be there for him; and Everyone couldn't always be.

And so he went around the world to find one or two maybe, depending on the supply of true friends. He did not find one, not even a single itty bitty one. (You and I were not part of this story back then, so we weren't found by him either.) Of course, there was the matter of his being very choosy too, as one must be while making true friends.

Marley found out that wherever it is that true friends are made, the supply was evidently down. As we all know, the invisible hand of the market had shooed them all away. Now who can argue with an invisible hand? I certainly couldn't, nor could Old Man Marley.

Supply only matches demand, so it has been said. Adam Smith said it. He must have been a wise man to know all this and must have had a lot of true friends back then when the world was a simpler place.

So, Old Man Marley went back home and thought to be proactive about his problems, the way people are, as is mentioned on any good curriculum vitae these days. He went about solving for the absence of a true friend.

He found a bunch of empty diaper boxes (size 6, mind you), and juxtaposed them to create his own true friend. Then he placed a bag of his choicest beans to weigh the friend's head a little bit so he would nod at everything that Marley said. Not because he agreed to what Marley said all the time, but because he approved of what he said as a matter of expression and acknowledgment. Marley called him True Friend Boxy, for obvious reasons.

Old Man Marley and T.F. Boxy would spend many evenings out on the patio, slurping tea. The more contemplative the topics, the slurpier was their tea drinking. They even took photos and posted them on the app that lets you look at people's faces all the time for entertainment.

The two would often sit together to meditate. And as all true friends have things in common, they both aspired to be empty boxes. Marley envied Boxy, secretly, for his apparent advantage there.

One fine day, there was a strong wind and True Friend Boxy's head was blown away. To Marley's horror, the beans that he had placed in there, spilled. The Old Man, understandably, was very upset that his true friend had spilled the beans. But, well, what could one do except gather them up and place them back in there and make sure that next time, True Friend Boxy was protected from strange head-blowing-away winds? Those winds were dangerous. They could mess up anyone's head, and badly so.

The following afternoon they were found sitting outdoors and enjoying some tea again when the wind picked up as is usual in windier places. Old Man Marley quickly held up his hands around Boxy's head, as if the head were a candle's burning wick with a flame so flickering. He held his hands up as long as the wind blew and thereby prevented a great loss.

Marley learned that even if your true friend is a box, he needs you as much as you need him — unless he is a volleyball, and that can only happen in movies, not real life.

The Book that Did Not Want to be Read

In a creative streak, Old Man Marley, once upon a time, decided to write a book. He chose his characters very carefully and lovingly. He imagined great adventures of a valiant prince, his trusted steed and the mouse in the house, and a few common folk here and there.

But as it happened, once Marley got done with writing, the characters were not happy with their parts. They failed to understand their necessary role in the completion of the story. So the horse didn't care about being a horse and wanted to be a mouse instead. The mouse wanted to be the prince and the prince was just plain bored and didn't want to proceed any further. Meanwhile, all the common folk just wanted to be the prince.

Even as he had the story written, the characters were running amok and not following along. Some of them wanted to roll off the page while others just didn't want to continue onto the next page. Can you ever imagine reading such a book?

"No no, please thank you," they said, as if refusing a cup of tea. "We are very comfortable right here by this full-stop."

The common folk characters just argued a lot, so much so that Marley didn't want to visit their pages anymore since they were beginning to give him a headache. Since they didn't hold the power to flip the pages, some of the characters denied the existence of all the pages beyond page 21. They all thought page 21 was where they must forever belong and so they all gathered there, ignoring pages 22–271. Now how could Marley explain to them, without giving away the ending, that they all couldn't be on the same page?

What was happening on page 17 was the scariest! The characters had decided to revolt. They didn't know what they were revolting against, as is common in common folk elsewhere. They caused the page to turn into a big dark blot of ink on paper. It did not  make sense at all. So Marley asked some of the characters why they weren't letting the book be read so the story could move on.

The characters simply replied:

"We did not ask to be written in this language of yours. We wanted it to be written in Chinese along with a smattering of African proverbs! And this red on the cover is gross, it has to be orange and blue."

To this, Marley sat with his head bent low, clasped in both hands. He didn't speak any Chinese or know any African adages! He thought about Hans Christian Andersen, and whether he had the same problems while writing, or if Shakespeare had to convince Juliet to be Juliet and not Romeo.

It had seemed so simple: write a book with characters in it; Everyone reads the book; and the end. Instead, it had turned into a circus full of clowns — and even that seemed more scripted than what his characters were up to.

Marley ultimately did what he had to do to wrap up the book. He gave a final explanation to all the characters. He explained that they would all be free to be whosoever they wished to be once they reached the end. But they must first go through the story as he wrote it, to be set free.

Those who understood went along happily and helped Marley finish the story by explaining the plot to those who didn't understand, and dragging them along by their tiny toes. And those who didn't care to learn were simply glued in after being carefully arranged, with a pair of tweezers, on the pages they belonged. It was only natural that they felt stuck, but the story was already written and each willingly or unwillingly had to play their parts. The horse, the mouse, the common folk and the bored prince. So it goes.

"C'est la vie," thought Marley, as he wiped his brow after a long day of work. "C'est la vie." And so Marley shut the book he had written and went to fix himself some hot tea and some Gladvil.

For "To-be-found"

I have to tell you the story of Marley going off digging by himself. Everyday he would start at 7:00 a.m. at the ocean's beach. He would take his shovel and move sand and dirt around digging, digging, digging. People became very curious about this activity and wondered what he was up to. So Everyone asked him:

"Old man! Wat'choo diggin' for?"

Old Man Marley, continued to dig in silence moving dirt around, swirling it with his spade, and pausing every now and then to look closely for something. Just when Everyone was about to turn and walk away, Marley exclaimed:

"I dig, for it to be found!" And Everyone, very confused, responded: "You mean you dig to find something?"

Marley responded: "No, to be found — I dig." He continued: "I dig for that pearl that will find me."

He took his shovel and moved dirt and sand around and around until he spotted something shiny. He picked it up and held it out for all to see before cradling it preciously in his palms and proclaiming:

"It is a thing of beauty to find, but even more so to be found. The pearl has found me even as I found it."

THE UNITED STATES

Everyone: Where do you live?
Old Man Marley: The United States.
Everyone: The United States of America?
Old Man Marley: No — The United States of Love.
Everyone: Where is that?
Old Man Marley: Inside.

And so Everyone went off to discover the land of the United States of this conundrum. And there they are to this day. So it happened. It did indeed.

Zombie Apocalypse

Old Man Marley woke up very early one morning to get a head start.

Marley had the world to himself all that time since Everyone else was asleep. He decided to accomplish so much more than one could imagine when Everyone else got in the way.

He read the histories of France and Germany simultaneously. Then he proceeded to rewrite it all, counterfactually. He proofread all his friends' posts and comments on various posts on social media, fact-checked them, and sent in his edits. He dotted all the T's and crossed all the I's everywhere! Yes, that is exactly what he did, and in that order too. He ran five miles to the left and then another five to the right — one may argue he got zero work done, as he returned to the same state of rest at the end as the one in which he began.

Finally, he decided to jump from plane to plane to experience various wonders until it was time to be confined by time and space.

Sadly, as the day proceeded, Marley found no one else was awake. This was a zombie apocalypse. The kind you know you're in, too — otherwise you wouldn't be reading this. Everyone carried tiny bosses guiding them with their eyes open and tricking them into keeping their minds shut, telling them what to eat, where to eat, and how much time to spend and where.

Everything was told to them by these tiny bosses they held in their hands all the time, or sometimes carefully placed in their pockets. If someone did not have their tiny boss with them, they would cower in the corner with anxiety, not knowing what to do next or whom to say what to.

People were so afraid of these tiny bosses. Wouldn't you be too? Imagine you put your hand in your pocket and find your actual boss right there in your pocket, typing out memos on your behavior. Hell, you'd be afraid of reaching in your pocket out of fear of grabbing your boss accidentally by the ear or nose. Or what if you pull out their mustache while retrieving them? And they're there all the time! It's really very stressful.

Oh, brain!

What a bad sight it was for Marley to see. He thought a head start in this day and age wasn't worth all that much when what it really all meant was loneliness and ever greater loneliness. That was worse than Marley's worst nightmare of being tickled by a giant octopus!

Marley was so afraid of the signs of the times that he crept back in bed and slid under the covers.

"Goodnight, Alexa!" he said. And he went back to sleep.

Nearly Otherworldly Experience

One fine day, Everyone woke up to find a strange humanlike object orbiting the earth at great speed. All they could hear from their vantage point was a very faint sound that sounded something like someone enjoying a merry-go-round of sorts: "Wheeeeeeeeeeeeeeeeeeeeeeee!" and then sudden silence. And then another "Wheeeeeeeeeeeeeeeeeee!" and then a sudden silence to be broken by another "wheeing" an hour later.

They took out their binoculars, telescopes, stethoscopes, kaleidoscopes, or whatever else people use within their means to scope out the reality of a situation these days.

Zooming into the source of the noise, they found that it was indeed Old Man Marley. (The ones with the kaleidoscopes of course remained very clueless, but they did indeed enjoy the converging patterns and colors that emerged and pretty much forgot what they were looking for.) It was him at 11:11 pm, 2:22 pm, and 3:33 pm appearing at the same point in the sky every hour. Circling the earth unendingly, or so it seemed.

Everyone asked someone to lasso Marley, and so he was plucked out of the orbit and brought back to Earth. Given the great speeds at which he was orbiting, Marley of course hit the ground running, and soon he was running around in circles, as was characteristic of anyone pursuant of anything in this world. The circles began to converge on a single point until finally, he was able to stop. He bowed down and marked the ground with a big X, before exclaiming, with his arms spread out as if he had just taken a bow:

"Hello, Everybodies! I'm here now!!"

Everyone was puzzled at such a declaration of nonchalance and pursued Marley to explain himself. How on earth did he manage to haul himself into outer space and get stuck in the orbit, and how long had he stayed there wheeing and revolving like a Marley-shaped moon? They had so many questions.

Marley removed his gloves. Then he removed his goggles and looked at Everyone with great delight as if he had just mastered the greatest secrets of the universe that had allowed him to exit time and space. This made Everyone even more curious.

"Old Man, what have you been up to today?"

Marley explained patiently and with enough hand gestures that had it been a work-out, would have amounted to roughly a 300 KJ of calorie burn an hour. He proceeded to draw huge circles with his arms, explaining to Everyone why he was found as he was stuck outside the world as it was — in an orbit, too. Some people thought this was some form of a Tai Chi fitness class and followed Marley's gestures for the added benefit, not paying attention to what was being said but following only what they saw.

It was not for any other reason but simply that every now and then, there will arise in Everyone a thirst to experience something extraordinary. For Marley, that something turned out to be an otherworldly experience. He had planned his escape carefully. Then he had entered the coordinates of "Other-world" into his trusted Doodle Maps and off he went.

The pull of the world, however, was very strong, he said. "Gravity and all!" he said. It was hard to get past a certain point, and then he ran out of fuel and got caught just far enough but not so far as to be able to make the exit. But stepping far enough also meant that there was hardly a way back, and so he was stuck in orbit. With nothing else to do, Marley began to take each circumambulation one orbit at a time, carefully avoiding being hit by space debris, and making friends with the stars while he was at it.

Everyone tried to follow what Marley was saying amid the frantic hand gestures. Everyone nodded in dismay. The others just continued to perform Tai Chi — true to the nature of their otherness.

Moral of the story:
When out to seek an otherworldly experience,
have enough fuel to carry on

A Very Ordinary Biography

Once again and upon a time, Old Man Marley decided to write a book. This book would be different from the book he had written earlier which could not be read because of character malfunction. Instead, it was going to be very readable because it was a story of his life — a biography. Of course, without much ado, Everyone took it upon their shoulders to try to convince Marley on why and how his book would not sell, or even get published.

"You're not rich or famous! Who wants to read about Old Man Marley and his silly shenanigans?" they said.

tap tap tap tap tap tap click click click tap tappety tap tap tap

Everyone was met with a pair of Marley's twinkling eyes from behind moon-shaped reading glasses, full of the joy of writing something plain and simple. Marley simply smiled away — that smile which could disarm any adversary of any stature, be he Brobdingnagian or Lilliputian.

Everyone turned to talk among themselves, as they normally did, to make themselves feel better about things that they themselves would not want to do, though equally capable.

"That Old Man Marley! His name doesn't even include an exclamation point like that guy Elon Muchfuss!, or that famous founder who founded Books with Faces, Marc Sugarplum. No. No. No. Marley is no founder of great things, who'd want to read about him?"

It was true. The only thing that Old Man Marley had ever founded was his own self — and of course, the pearl that he had dug out years ago.

click click tap tap tappety tap tap.

Finally, after several days, Marley emerged flapping his arms excitedly like a hen that had just laid an egg. One could take a moment and appreciate how hens must pride themselves in that miraculous feat of laying an egg, to be that excited about it. If only we could all see the sunny side up in everything and then make a huge fuss about it so others could see it too.

So it goes, that curiosity cracks the egg — and Everyone quickly began to order their copies of Marley's great biography. To Everyone's surprise, it was remarkable how relatable it all was. They had seen it all happen before their very eyes. It was equally a story of their own lives almost as if Marley had ended up writing a biography of them by writing his own.

Everyone was all filled with tears and with laughter at being reminded of how they had once woken up to see their streets all painted blue and covered with confused zebras that now had purple hearts on them. Or how Dusty would invite them all over for a dinner of mud pies every other week, and the time Marley fell in love and died and was reborn to do it all over again.

Newspapers flashed headlines:

"Old Man writes extraordinary book on ordinary life"

"Ordinary life hot topic for rich and famous — million copies sold"

***

Finally, as Marley was invited to a book signing at the largest bookstore, Blab and Doodle (where he kindly requested a chair arrangement upside down from the ceiling for spatial considerations), lined up in the crowd right there with Everyone, were none other than Marc Sugarplum and Elon Muchfuss! with their own copies of Marley's book to be signed.

Such is life also. Sometimes.

BIGGEST PRESENT EVER

Once upon a time, Old Man Marley was to go to little Kiki's birthday party. He was very fond of her indeed and so he wanted to show his affection with a meaningful present.

However, meaning got lost when Everyone came up with something so big and fancy it was now hard to tell if it all had meaning to begin with. Marley wondered if people who love more, needed to give even bigger presents. It certainly didn't seem like thought counted anymore. Even if it did, it could only count till ten. Or even less. People have gadgets these days to do the counting for them.

Now, Old Man Marley was not a money-full person, although he was rich beyond measure, in the unconventional sense of the word, of course. So to solve this conundrum, he went about laying a step-by-step plan to give the biggest present ever or his name was not Marley — (which really it wasn't).

So to execute his plan, he went around buying a lot of gift wrapping paper. He bought out all the stores and warehouses selling those. He bought so much paper that the world became curious and newspapers began publishing stories:

"Old Man Rampant - Buying Wrapping Paper"

and…

"Epic Proportions of Wrapping Paper Bought by Man—Old Man."

"World Forced into Buying Tiny Presents for Lack of Enough Wrapping Paper"

And to the greatest horror of all:

"This Christmas: Only Love Will Have to Do—No Wrapped Presents."

Finally, it was the day that Kiki turned one. Everyone woke up and did not see the sun – all they saw was wrapping paper. Wrapping paper carefully wrapped around their houses, around chimneys, covering roads, all of Germany, France, and respectfully, England and over the oceans, to Canada, and so on.

Marley came around Antarctica and faced the problem of wrapping paper around the curvature but managed. Finally, after being done with all this wrapping he took a step back and admired his work. And with a proud smirk characteristic of one, very pleased with himself for all he accomplished overnight, he stuck the note he wrote to the little darling baby:

"Dear Kiki,

Tis the biggest gift in the world, on your birthday—The World itself.

For you to unwrap and discover for the rest of your life.

XOXO
Old Man"

The End.

Old Man Marley's Rest In Piece

"Ladies and Gentlemen

This is a public announcement. Today at 3:13 pm, on a sunny afternoon, Old Man Marley was laid to rest.

His final words were:

"I will be back!"

...

After After-Life

Everyone woke up one morning to find a gigantic sunflower blocking their sunlight. The plant, of course, grew right where they had buried Marley, and just like how he used to be, God bless his heart, the flower was in their face. But of course, Everyone thought — Marley must be pulling otherworldly tricks on them — even right while he was in the Great Beyond.

Everyone gathered to chop down the gigantic sunflower that was causing such dysfunction. That's when they noticed right under the enormous sunflower was a gigantic pod slowly beginning to unwrap its petals.

Voila! Right before their eyes, there was a second sunflower — and who should be sitting smack in the center of it —the good Old Man Marley!— all dapper with his newspaper held upside down and sipping his otherworldly tea-looking very much alive and …well…rested. Everyone's jaw dropped — the same as would yours if you saw someone raised from the dead in such, let's say, flowery fashion, for he had literally flowered back to life.

Old Man lifted his head. As soon as he saw Everyone, his expressions turned to joy. He climbed down as if he were boarding off an airplane. His booming voice broke the awe-struck silence:

"I missed you all! Come here, Everyone — I give you all a big hug!"

Curiously, as soon as Marley stepped off the plant, the flowers dried up and fell back into the grave, freeing up the sunlight. Such is life also: throws bigger problems your way to make the smaller ones disappear by themselves — even if momentarily they're blocking all of your sunlight.

Everyone gasped and now stood quite pale with confusion and a lack of understanding:

"But….. but … Old Man … we buried you," they exclaimed.

"Ah, you see, you're thinking about this all wrong," Marley responded "— You didn't bury me; you planted me right back, and here I am — as I promised I would be. Isn't that what happens when you plant things in the soil? They grow back."

Everyone retorted in unison: "But— you died!"

"Nonsense!" Marley snapped. He paused briefly while donning a rather matter-of-fact expression, "The living cannot die. Only the dead die."

Clearly, all of this was totally bananas to Everyone — in fact, they would have preferred bananas popping out of sunflowers over all this any day.

They tried their very best to follow. If they were attending modern schools these days- they'd all be given tiny trophies for achieving the perfect attempt, even if unsuccessful. Their parents would be so proud of their confounded little monkeys. You see, the thing with modern schools is they don't want anyone to "get it," which is why they historicize, socialize, theorize, and politicize — and if you ask too many questions, they send you off to exercise. Now, where were we:

"Alright then, looks like it's all settled. I've got lots to do and half the time to do it in," Marley exclaimed as he straightened up and dusted his lapel.

One would have imagined that Old Man Marley could have returned a lot younger looking — but no — he appeared the same as when they sowed him — err planted —err buried into the ground. Except for one thing only — his feet appeared to be a lot bigger now. Wonder where he'd find the shoes to fit those huge feet? Did soles that size even exist?

Everyone responded: "Marley, why are you in such a rush — you just bloomed — we have so many questions — existential questions…stay a while!"

"Opportunity hardly ever knocks twice, and when it does — you better run with it," Marley raised his index finger high for emphasis before continuing: "Now, excuse me, I must hurry — I must find a wife, a job, a fine china cup for my tea … and in any order…. You see, I have a list - it's all in here.."

And surely it was — a long scroll was trailing behind as if all this time Marley spent in the after-life, he was ruminating over what he wanted to be doing in the after-after-life.

"But, as the first order of business, I must find my residence!" and with those words, Marley darted off.

What would you call this occurrence then, other than weird!? Certainly, it wasn't a birth — nor a born-again. Was this how Marley came to the world originally? Is this why no one knew how old he really was? It started to make sense — somewhat.

Regardless...

Moral of the story:
If you find yourself planted, bloom, shamelessly!

FIBER

Old Man Marley was faring seemingly better this time around, Everyone thought. He seemed to be talking about and doing all the right things that Everyone felt he should be doing, like the occasional worry and mention about fiber and the weather, for instance. He was even found sitting by his window ruminating quietly — the way older adults are expected to do — smoking absolutely nothing.

However, now that Marley seemed to be — well-functioning like any normal adult should be — the world was all topsy-turvy. Everyone was wearing masks, running away from each other like they had some communicable disease. As if that weren't enough, people decided to go to war for no apparent reason, and so on. Elon "Muchfuss!" wasn't making any fuss these days, and nor was Mark Sugarplum — even though now they finally had plenty of legitimate reasons to do so. Bill's gates were no longer together, so one couldn't expect much from him. In fact, after a union of more than 20 years, his gates had decided to open and shut in different ways - there was going to be no closure in this situation whatsoever.

And poor old Jeff Heuvos— he was laying low — very, very low —behind a pile of soon-to-be-shipped boxes — lost in oblivion.

Marley thought the giants of the current century seemed a lot little, especially how little they were actually contributing to the fiber of society and humanity. True, they were no politicians and perhaps didn't know right from wrong as much as politicians did - it was probably pointless to expect much there.

It was as if while Marley slept, the world had lost its bearings.

How little did Everyone focus on fiber, Marley thought — the actual thing that mattered to keep everything going in the true sense. If only people began to up their intake of what's real and what really matters — the world would be a very different place. At the minimum, they would have enough to regulate everything else that comes in and goes out - like money, fame, power, and economic crisis - among other by-products of human functioning.

It takes great discernment to separate the fluff from fiber, Marley thought. These days they all come mixed together in very attractive packaging. The fluffier, the more attractive the packaging. One has to really pay attention to the ingredients otherwise Everyone was consuming ingredients that they were unaware of — like sugar-coated fiber — that was the worstestest! Or how about the Corny Flakes that boast about sugar that tastes just like fiber! Marley nodded away his disapproval by himself — and nearly gagged thinking of the taste of such a thing.

Moral to soluble — Marley understood how important fiber was to hold the society and the human body together. Like truth, it was hard on digestion for sure — but once through, it really brought out the best in Everyone, especially when they realized that they all had the same basic needs. It was all interconnected — every system, so the basic necessities needed to be right and amply available.

Over his bowl of overnight oats for breakfast, Marley decided it was time to roll up his sleeves and do something about it himself. The rest of his list could wait. Everyone deserves a chance to experience what true fiber tastes like at least once in their lifetime(s). Marley hoped, once they tasted it, they would never go back to all that fluff or, in the least, would have the discernment that's needed to process what's written under the flap of a Mind-U-bar.

***

The next day, Everyone woke up with the town covered in fliers. Fliers everywhere — even in their breakfast bowls of corny flakes and sugary drone-ola down to their socks and shoes — fliers were popping out of every nook and cranny. Everyone looked up at the sky in dismay to find tons of fliers raining down from an airplane— and who should be aboard the aircraft — of course, yours truly Old Man Marley.

Carefully sprawled across each edible and extremely fibrous flier were the words: Bite me!

And Everyone did — the way they ought to when served with the Truth. Needless to say, it was the release that Everyone had been looking for all their lives. One day humanity would look back and thank Marley for the enlightenment.

Moral of the story: Bite into truth, not dust.

Marley's Internet Disconnection

Once upon a time, Old Man Marley lost his internet connection,

There he was, sitting as he was, with his laptop upon a table and a chair,

The internet just wouldn't connect, oh no it would not, almost as if it wasn't event there,

The conundrum that faced him, was a one-password-key that effaced him,

Now the old man sat, helping himself to recall the carefully crafted mnemonic,

As he thoughtfully reclined back in a setting, nicely ergonomic,

Flibbertigibbet, rumpfedranjyon,

Unabhaengigkeitsdeklaration?

And so he muttered all sorts of Shakespearean gibberish, of course, and some German (with no relation),

Everyone who came to help him,

Explained he needed some time,

All to find out the key to his connection, and some meaning, perhaps reason to this pointless rhyme,

"Pointless!" exclaimed Marley, "Nothing is not!"
"I only have some trouble with a password that I forgot!"
"The implications are rather simple,"
He dabbed his finger thoughtfully against his dimple,
"If I have no connection, there is no point of this hi-tech equipment,
To end my problems, I will make one minor adjustment,"
With this, Marley shut his laptop and with it, stood up to walk away,
Everyone shuffled after him to see what next he was to do and say,
"My dear Everyone, Alexa and Sir-ee,"
He addressed then all, rather respectfully,
"I thank you all and I need you all not anymore,"
"The world is wide open today, for me to step out and explore some more,"
"But Marley," everyone in unison loudly elicited a shout,
"You still need your doodle maps, or GPS to chart your route!"
Marley gave his chest a little double-click, and his head a little artful sway,
"I trust my heart will help me find the way!"

The End